THE

ADVENTURES

From the makers of Doctor Who

BBC CHILDREN'S BOOKS

Published by the Penguin Group
Penguin Books Ltd, 80 Strand, London WC2R 0RL, England
Penguin Group (USA) Inc., 375 Hudson Street, New York, New York 10014, USA
Penguin Group (Australia) Ltd, 250 Camberwell Road, Camberwell, Victoria, 3124, Australia
(a division of Pearson Australia Group Pty Ltd)
Canada, India, New Zealand, South Africa

Published by BBC Children's Books, 2007
Text and design © Children's Character Books, 2007

10 9 8 7 6 5 4 3 2 1

Sarah Jane Adventures © BBC 2007

BBC logo ™ & BBC 1996. Licensed by BBC Worldwide Limited

ISBN 978-1-40590-399-8

Printed in the United Kingdom

THE

Sarah Jane

ADVENTURES

From the makers of Doctor Who

Eye of the Gorgon

Written by Phil Ford

Based on the script by Phil Ford

'I saw amazing things, out there in space. But there's strangeness to be found wherever you turn. Life on Earth can be an adventure, too.

You just have to know where to look.'

SARAH JANE SMITH

Chapter One

The nun

It was the owl that woke her. Not a gentle hoot carried through her open window on the still air of a warm summer's night, but the screech of a barn owl.

Edith Randall woke with a start.

It had been six months since she had finally given in to the worries and the arguments with her children and sold the family home to move to Lavender Lawns.

Lavender Lawns Rest Home for the Elderly.

She wasn't elderly, she had told Mark and Jenny the first time they told her the name of the home. And even if she was just a *little* bit older than she used to be, she certainly didn't need to rest. But, to be honest, even the first time they had brought the brochures along to show her, a little part of Edith had liked the look of the place. It was a very grand old house with wide, rolling lawns and stately trees. The rooms were nice and, while she wouldn't be able to bring everything from the house that she had shared with her husband for almost fifty years, she would be able to keep the things that mattered. The things that reminded her of him, and of their shared joy in raising two such wonderful children.

Oh, she hadn't given in straight away. A person's independence means a lot to them. A person's roots and memories mean more. But she secretly kept the Lavender Lawns brochure in her sideboard drawer, and occasionally she would look at it and tempt herself with the idea...

And six months ago she had moved in. It had been everything that her children and the brochure said it would be. She had her own personal space, her own things around her, she had made new friends, she had apple crumble with thick, warm custard every Thursday, and bingo and singalongs every Saturday.

Apparently, there was also the ghost of a nun. But she didn't pay any mind to that. Some of her new friends had over-active imaginations. Sometimes, as age slowed up their bodies, people took some pretty wild flights of fancy. Bless them! Not everyone at Lavender Lawns still kept all their marbles in the tin. She didn't worry about the talk of the ghostly nun that some of them had seen in their rooms.

But the barn owl screeched somewhere in the night, and Edith woke up. Someone else was in the room with her.

'Hello? Who's there?'

It could have been one of the care staff, she thought. Perhaps in her sleep she had caught the bright orange emergency cord that hung by her bed and pulled it.

'Who is it?'

And out of the darkness moved a tall, cowled figure.

The nun!

Edith gasped for breath, her heart hammering as her hand searched frantically for the switch to her bedside light, all her doubts about the Lavender Lawns ghost evaporating in one blood-freezing moment. Her thumb found the toggle of the light switch. Soft light spilled through the pink tasselled lampshade, across the bed and into the darkness of the room.

The nun had vanished.

Chapter Two

The promise

'My an and Mrs Randall go back forever. She used to live next door 'til her old feller died.'

Clyde Langer was sitting on the back seat of the powder blue Nissan Figaro as it swept along the narrow country lanes that would – so it said on the ten-year-old map resting on the drive's lap – lead them to the Lavender Lawns rest home.

Sarah Jane Smith didn't let things like an out-of-date road atlas worry her. She had travelled through time and space; she didn't think she'd have any trouble getting from Ealing to Lavender Lawns with an old map book and a degree of educated guesswork. It didn't matter that back home in her attic, Sarah Jane had an alien computer that was probably more powerful than top-secret government equipment. She just didn't see the need of satellite navigation. Sarah Jane was a journalist, and when she got the scent of a story, she didn't even need pointing in the right direction.

'Nan says there's no way Mrs Randall sees things, or makes things up,' said Clyde. He was fourteen, lean, but big for his age, and big for the back seat of the little car.

'And it's not just her that's been scared by this ghostly nun? Other residents have seen it, too?'

Sarah Jane was looking at Clyde in the rear-view mirror. She saw as much as heard him grunt a confirmation.

Beside her, another boy said, 'I thought there was no such thing as a ghost.'

Sarah Jane glanced at him and smiled, 'Maybe that's what we're about to find out.'

The other boy, Luke, was slighter than Clyde, with a thick mane of brown hair and dark eyes. He could have been Sarah Jane's son. That's what she called him and she had the adoption papers to prove it. But he wasn't. He looked like he was fourteen, like Clyde. But he wasn't that, either. The truth was that Luke hadn't been born; he'd been developed as part of an alien plan to turn Earth's population into food for a nasty tentacled species called the Bane. Luke's part in their plan hadn't worked out all that well, thanks largely to Sarah Jane and her young neighbour Maria Jackson. Together they had defeated the Bane and rescued naïve but intelligent Luke– the son Sarah Jane had always longed for without realizing it.

Clyde hadn't been around then. He had shown up later, for the Slitheen. His cold chip sandwiches had been vital in beating them.

Aliens had been part of Sarah Jane's life for a long, long time. As she took the turn into the gates of Lavender Lawns she thought a ghost – if such a thing existed – would make a nice change.

When they arrived at Lavender Lawns, a care assistant showed them up to Edith Randall's room. If she'd had a fright a couple of nights before, she didn't look like she was letting it get her down, thought Sarah Jane. She suspected that Edith Randall had even had her hair done for the interview. Sarah Jane smiled and did the introductions. It didn't take much persuasion to get all the information out of her.

'Nora Connelly was the first to see the nun. She'd been to the loo – terrible trouble with her waterworks, she has. Three or four times every night.'

Sarah Jane didn't take the details down. Luke and Clyde both grinned. By now Clyde was running a bemused eye over Edith's Toby jug collection. Luke was at the window, watching the old folk in the garden. Some of them were chattering, going for a stroll with Zimmer frames and walking sticks, others just sat there and soaked up the late summer sun. Some of them, he thought, looked strangely lifeless. He could see their eyes were open – he could tell they weren't dead – and yet it was like something about them was.

'Anyway,' Edith Randall was saying, 'she comes out of the bathroom, and there she was – the nun – by her chest of drawers.'

'Fainted like a schoolgirl. No constitution, at all. Surprising, amount of times she's been married.'

'And has anyone come up with any idea why this nun haunts the place?'

'Not that I've heard. I didn't believe a word of it, 'til I saw it myself. I'm more level-headed, you know.'

'I see.'

She smoothed down her hair. 'So will there be a photographer? You wouldn't think it, but I was in all the papers once. Miss Ealing, 1951.'

Luke and Clyde caught each other's eye – *no way!*

Luke looked back out of the window – and found one of the elderly women out there staring straight back at him. Something about that look made him uncomfortable. But he didn't look away, and neither did she. He couldn't have said how old she was – somehow, when you came into the world the way he did, it was tough trying to judge the age of other people. But her hair was silver, she was slender and straight-backed – although she used a stick – and he supposed that years ago she might have been beautiful. Then, quite suddenly she stopped looking at him. It wasn't so much that she looked away, as that she seemed to forget about him. She began to walk away, as Luke watched, it looked as if she was talking to herself.

Sarah Jane wound up the interview with Edith Randall telling her she'd let her know about the photographer. Right now she had to go and talk to the Lavender Lawns manager.

'Oh, her,' said Edith. She clearly wasn't a fan.

'Yes. Mrs Gribbins. Don't you like her?'

'Oh, she runs this place all right, I suppose.'

'It is a lovely place to live,' said Sarah Jane.

'I just think she's a bit shifty, that's all.'

'Shifty? I'll bear that in mind.'

Edith suddenly worried, 'Don't say I said so, will you?'

'Don't you worry. Not a word.'

Edith relaxed, and smiled. Her eyes fell on Clyde, 'Now, I've got a couple of little jobs for you. Your grandma said you wouldn't mind.'

Clyde's jaw dropped and Luke slapped him on the shoulder, grinning as he made his escape with Sarah Jane.

Mrs Gribbins was, apparently, in the home's separate recreational block and as Sarah Jane and Luke emerged from the house into the sunshine, Luke cast a look over the home's residents again. Still walking, talking or just sitting there. Nothing seemed to move on very quickly at Lavender Lawns.

He looked from a couple of old gents playing a game of chess on a small picnic table to Sarah Jane, 'When do people get old?'

She looked at him and smiled. It was a good question.

'The lucky ones never seem to. Then there are others that act like they were born drawing a pension.'

'I don't understand.'

'It's not so much about the lines on your face. It's more a state of mind.'

As they walked, they passed a woman in a wheelchair with the glazed look that Luke had seen on other residents. Sarah Jane felt a stab of sorrow.

'Sometimes, though,' she said, 'people don't have a choice about how they get old. Sometimes the people they used to be, they're just not there any more.'

Luke was frowning. Some things about life and death didn't have clear explanations. Sarah Jane ran a hand through his hair. Fleetingly, she wondered if Luke would ever have to worry about things like old age and dementia. She wondered if he would still be around to look after her.

'Look,' she said, diverting herself from thoughts of getting old, 'why don't you take a wander around the grounds while I talk to the manager. Let me know if you spot any nuns walking through walls.'

Luke smiled, 'See you back at the car.'

He watched as Sarah Jane made her way towards the recreation block, then turned and saw the old woman he'd seen earlier staring at him. She seemed to be talking to herself again, and he couldn't resist getting closer to hear what she was saying.

'The Colonel wouldn't believe us, darling,' she told some invisible companion. Her voice was clear, and strong. What he'd heard kids at school describe as posh.

Luke was fascinated. Who was the Colonel?

'Who would believe us?' she continued, walking steadily with the aid of her cane. 'Better to keep mum. Yes, better that way.'

Somehow she missed her footing, stumbled, but Luke quickly reached out a steadying hand.

'Are you all right?'

The woman straightened up quickly. 'Yes, yes. Quite all right,' she said and Luke got the clear impression that although she was old and clearly needed care (why else would she be here?) there was something about her that was fiercely independent.

Then she looked at him closely. 'Are you one of

the...' she was struggling hard to find the word... 'one of the...Colonel's chaps?'

Luke shook his head, 'No.'

Then she smiled. It was a wonderful thing that lit up her face, and made her young and beautiful again.

'I'm Bea Nelson-Stanley. I'm looking for my husband, the Professor. He said to meet him between the paws of the...oh, what's it called? The blessed thing! The paws of the Sphinx.'

Luke didn't understand, 'That's in Egypt. This is England.'

Then Luke saw something happen. He wasn't sure what it was. Something about her face, or something in her eyes. But something changed. And it seemed as if she was seeing him clearly for the first time.

'You're the boy in the window,' she said.

'My name's Luke. We were visiting Mrs Randall. She says this place is haunted by a nun. Have you seen her?'

Bea's mouth tightened into a grim line, 'I have. But she's no ghost.'

Luke was going to ask her what the nun was, then – but Bea was staring at him, intent.

'There's something different about you, Luke.'

He felt himself take a step backwards.

Bea smiled reassuringly and took his hand, 'Don't be afraid. It's all right. I've met...unusual... people before. Perhaps you can help me.'

'How? How can I help you?' Luke wanted to know.

But Bea was already using the cane to move on. Luke watched her. Despite the cane her steps were confident. But Luke wasn't all that confident that the old lady – no matter how nice she seemed – wasn't entirely mad.

Then she stopped and turned to look at him, 'Are you coming or not?'

And Luke found he couldn't resist. Clyde would probably say Bea was nutty as a plumber's tool box (Clyde had said that once about him) but Clyde wasn't there, and Luke had a feeling that just maybe it had something to do with the nun.

So Luke went with Bea and, as he did so, Sarah Jane watched Sylvia Gribbins stare down her almost-impossibly long nose at the business card she had just handed over.

'A reporter?' said Mrs Gribbins. For someone in a caring profession she sneered very easily.

'I'm looking into the story of a ghostly nun

haunting the rest home. I understand quite a few residents have seen it.'

Sarah Jane watched Mrs Gribbins pocket the business card and sneer again. They were in the recreation room. A couple of residents were involved in a game of table tennis that Sarah Jane would have sworn she was watching in slow motion.

'Might I suggest you try Westminster for something rather more newsworthy, Miss Smith?'

'You don't believe Lavender Lawns is haunted, then?'

Mrs Gribbins shook her head impatiently. Sarah Jane was signing up fast with Edith Randall on the subject of the Lavender Lawns manager.

'One old dear has a nightmare, she tells her friend she's seen a ghost, and what do you know? Next thing, they're all seeing one.

'It's hysteria, Miss Smith. It's as simple as that.'

Sarah Jane ran her eyes over the few residents in the recreation room. They looked happy enough, but who knew for sure? She looked back at Mrs Gribbins, and felt a little angry.

'Perhaps,' she said. 'Or maybe it's a cry for

attention.'

Sarah Jane enjoyed the flash of anger in Mrs Gribbins' eye.

'Thank you for your time, Mrs Gribbins. I'll find my own way out.'

Sarah Jane left the recreation room, biting down on a tide of anger inside her. Whether or not ghosts existed, how could a woman like Mrs Gribbins dismiss the very real worries of the people in her care like that? She found Clyde waiting by the car – and his mood wasn't much better.

Mrs Randall had had him turning her mattress, moving Toby jugs around on the top shelf so she could see them better, hunting under her bed for a lost slipper.

'I came here looking for spooks, not jobs,' he complained. 'Why is it old people always want you to do everything for them?'

Sarah Jane was already annoyed by Mrs Gribbins; she didn't need Clyde's whining. 'We all get old, Clyde,' she told him dismissively. 'Even you.'

'Not me. Way technology's going, by the time I'm forty I can get my brain put in a robot and live for ever.'

Sarah Jane looked at him and shook her head in despair. Once, in what seemed like another lifetime, she had come across a race that had done just that, and thought they could take over the universe. They had been called Cybermen.

It was too nice a day to think about them.

'Have you seen Luke?' she asked.

But Clyde hadn't. Luke was still with Bea. She had led him almost to the edge of the grounds, and a big old yew tree. There she had handed him her stick and told him they had to be quick – before anyone saw. When he asked her who might be watching she became nervous and frustrated as she fought and failed to find the right words...

'I have these...holes,' she gasped, rapping her head with long, elegant fingers.

Holes in her head? thought Luke.

But Bea was now reaching up into the tree, into a crevice in the trunk. A moment later she withdrew her hand, holding something and Luke saw tears in her eyes.

'I knew they might find me one day,' she told him. 'But I couldn't be parted from it. Foolish old woman!'

And she handed him a small tin box. The lid was rusted tight. It had been years since the tin had been opened, but Luke managed it. Inside lay a talisman. A beautiful thing on a chain. It was obviously old, with a strange green gemstone at its heart. And as Luke touched it gently with his fingertips, a fire deep in the heart of the stone began to glow.

Luke gasped, 'What is it?'

Bea's eyes lit with the glow of the talisman, but she didn't touch it. Instead she looked around nervously.

'Just...promise me,' she struggled. 'Promise me you won't tell anyone that you have the talisman. And whatever you do – do not let her get it!'

And she grabbed Luke, her eyes – frightened and defiant – boring into his, 'Do not let her get it!'

'Who?'

'Put it away and promise me!'

Luke closed the tin and slid it into his pocket, 'I promise. But who's after it?'

But then Bea was only looking at him. Something like the change Luke had seen before had happened again. But now it was as if she didn't quite see him, didn't know him...

'It was nice to meet you, young man. But I really am very busy,' she said. And with that, she walked away. A moment later Luke caught her voice in the air. She was singing some old song about a slow boat to China.

Luke set off back towards the car. He guessed that Sarah Jane would probably be waiting for him by now. He wasn't so sure what to do about the talisman. The way it had glowed he had no doubt that it was alien. But he had made a promise to Bea to say nothing about it – and a promise, he had learned, was something you didn't break.

By the time he reached the car and found Sarah Jane and Clyde he had made up his mind to stay quiet – at least until he'd had chance to take a better look at the talisman.

Sarah Jane was eager to get going.

'So what's the story?' Clyde wanted to know. 'Is the place haunted or what?'

Mrs Gribbins stood in the doorway of the home watching as Sarah Jane turned the ignition and put the Figaro into gear. 'I don't know,' she said, eyeing Mrs Gribbins, 'but there's something about it here I don't like.'

As Sarah Jane swung the car out of the Lavender Lawns gates, Mrs Gribbins took from her pocket the business card Sarah Jane had given her. Mrs Gribbins was uneasy. Not just about the reporter's visit, but because she had seen Mrs Nelson-Stanley talking to one of the boys that had come with her. Curious, Mrs Gribbins had reached for the binoculars they kept in the recreation room for bird watching. She had seen Mrs Nelson-Stanley give the boy something.

And she knew it had to be what they had been looking for. It was the talisman for which the Sisters had been searching.

Chapter Three

Every girl needs her mum

Maria had been teaching her dad to bake when her mum showed up looking for a bed.

No, that wasn't like her mum. That wasn't Chrissie at all.

She showed up having fallen out with the boyfriend so now here she was, bags packed, *expecting* a bed.

That was Chrissie.

But no way was Maria going to let her walk back out of the kitchen door. She had seen her do that before – and that was how, a year later, she and her dad were living in Bannerman Road and Chrissie was shacked up with her smooth boyfriend Ivan on the other side of the city. That was until now, of course...

'It's Ivan's own stupid fault,' Chrissie told Alan, Maria's dad, as she stood in the doorway and dumped her bags on the kitchen floor.

'If he hadn't been spending so much time at that flaming office, I'd never have thought of going to salsa lessons, would I?'

'Salsa?' Alan was standing in the kitchen wearing an apron dusted with flour, one finger covered with cake mix scraped from the mixing bowl. He had been about to lick it off when the door burst open and there was Chrissie.

'Then Ivan gets the hump. Gets all possessive. And next thing I know, Carlos is on the ballroom floor with a bloody nose.'

Carlos was the salsa teacher.

'So, has Ivan got the push, then?' Alan asked.

'More of a nudge. Reminding him what he stands to lose if he doesn't sharpen up. You know, he even said I was having a mid-life crisis! Mid-life, cheek!'

Alan's eyes travelled to the suitcases. He was

getting a very bad feeling about all this.

'And you're planning to stay here?'

'Where else am I going to go?'

Alan was about to list some possibilities. But then Maria came back into the kitchen (she had gone to her room to grab a cookery book from school) and, of course, the issue was settled just like that.

'Mum!' she cried.

And they were hugging each other, and it was going to be just like old times. Only Alan knew it just wouldn't be. Chrissie wouldn't be staying. He didn't want her to. And that, in the end, was going to make life so much more complicated for everyone.

There were going to be tears, he knew it. And he wouldn't have to wait long. Chrissie arrived around 10 o'clock. They started a little after lunch.

Maria was lying on the floor in her bedroom, schoolbooks fanned around her, when Chrissie came in.

'Anything I can help with?' she asked.

Maria looked up and grinned, 'You and maths? I don't think so.'

Chrissie sat down on the bed. Maria was

right, when Chrissie had been at school the only figures she'd been interested in were guys' phone numbers.

'Maybe we can do something together after you've finished?' Chrissie suggested. 'Go into town, do some more maths on my credit cards?'

Maria smiled. It was good to have her back in the house again – even if, perhaps, it wasn't going to be for good. She and her mum used to have some good times together. She could remember when her parents had, too. A part of her hoped this break from Ivan and this stop-over in the new house at Bannerman Road would lead to something...on the other hand, Maria was a smart girl and life didn't tend to shape up the way it did in soaps.

Either way, she couldn't hit the shops with her mum that afternoon – she had said she'd see Sarah Jane.

And that was where the trouble started.

'Sarah Jane?' Chrissie echoed. It was funny how she made the name sound like something she'd stepped in. 'Come on, Maria, I'm your mum. What are you doing, always off gallivanting with those weirdos over the road?'

Maria tried to laugh it off, 'Sarah Jane and

Luke aren't weirdos.'

But Chrissie wasn't laughing, 'It's weird how much time you spend with her. And there's something about that boy – I hope you don't fancy him. I don't know what it is, but he's not right.'

If only she knew, thought Maria. But that didn't mean there was anything wrong with Luke – he was just different, that was all. Very different. Like, he didn't have a belly-button. You couldn't get much more different from everybody else than that, could you? All the same, Chrissie had no right to have a go at her friends like this...

'I'm telling you, Maria, there's some funny people in the world!'

And that was it! Maria was on her feet, homework forgotten, trips to the shops forgotten, any thought of her mum coming home for good forgotten. Maria seethed.

'You don't know anything about Sarah Jane and Luke!'

Chrissie almost reeled, 'I'm your mum, love. I'm only trying to protect you.'

'I don't need you to protect me!'

'Come on, darling, every girl needs her mum.'

And that was *really* it!

'Yeah?' Maria shouted at her mum. 'So how come you walked out on me, then?'

Chrissie felt that like a slap across the face. She even felt the tears spring to her eyes. Tears as real as the ones Maria was shedding.

'Maria,' she tried.

But Maria wasn't interested, 'Oh, just shut up!'

And she was out of there, slamming the bedroom door on her shell-shocked mum, and thundering down the stairs. She saw Alan waiting for her at the bottom of the stairs, alerted by the shouting and looking worried.

'What's going on, love?' he asked.

'She doesn't like me seeing Sarah Jane and Luke – like she knows anything about them!'

Alan put an arm around her shoulders, and pressed her close to him. He still carried on him the smell of their morning baking together.

'Look,' he said quietly, 'we'll be back to normal in a few days.'

Maria sniffed back her tears, wiped them away from an eye with the heel of her palm, 'You mean she'll be back with Ivan.'

Alan smiled, tried for a joke, 'If he doesn't see sense and do a runner while she's gone.'

A joke usually worked with Maria. But not today.

'Doesn't it bother you?'

Alan groaned inside. This was just what he'd been scared of when Chrissie turned up like that, and Maria had obviously been so keen that she should stay. Maria wanted her mum back. It was only natural. Only it was never going to happen.

'Your mum and me, Maria, you know that's all over. For good.'

Maria pulled away from her dad, and went off like a distress flare, 'Well, that's great for you, isn't it? Some solicitor gives you a bit of paper, and it's all over! What good's that to me, Dad? She's always going to be my mum!'

'Yes, I know that, sweetheart,' Alan said. He hated to see his daughter like this. He had hoped this was behind them, that she had come to terms with the end of the marriage. But maybe that would never happen, as long as Chrissie kept treating their new place as some kind of second home.

His heart broke as he saw fresh tears tumble down Maria's cheeks.

'Maybe I want her to get to know my friends, so she doesn't think they're weird anymore. Maybe I don't want her to go back to Ivan. But that's never going to happen, is it? Because you've got a piece of paper!'

'Maria...'

But she was already out of the front door. For a second he thought about chasing after her. But what was the point? It wasn't as if she had done anything wrong, was it? All she wanted was her family, her mum and dad. Deep in his heart, Alan knew that if anyone had done something wrong, it was him and Chrissie – they had let their daughter down.

Chapter Four

The Abbess

St Agnes' Abbey loomed over Sylvia Gribbins. It was a cold place, she thought. Built of dark grey granite with windows that seemed to watch you like big, black hooded eyes, it was a long way off anything in *The Sound of Music*. But then, Mrs Gribbins thought as she raised the heavy iron doorknocker and struck the riveted oak door, these nuns didn't remind her much of Julie Andrews, either.

One of them answered her knocking. She was a pale, thin woman and the black habit and wimple made her skin look even whiter. If Mrs Gribbins had woken in the middle of the night and found her standing in the shadows, even she might have believed in ghosts.

H 4 T R F G 8 N D 1 S W O B X O 3 T R 2 U F S 7 K

'I've come to see Sister Helena,' said Mrs Gribbins.

The pale nun said nothing, but opened the door for Mrs Gribbins to go in. She wasn't surprised or offended by the nun's silence, she had visited the abbey only twice before, but neither time had anyone spoken to her apart from Sister Helena. Vows of silence, she supposed.

It had been Sister Helena who approached Mrs Gribbins in the first place, shortly after she had taken over at Lavender Lawns. She hadn't really relished the idea of visiting the abbey at Sister Helena's invitation that first time; running Lavender Lawns didn't allow a lot of time for socializing with nuns. But maybe the abbey wanted to offer some sort of help with running the place? Forty-five elderly residents complete with Zimmer frames and dietary problems could be quite a handful. Any offers of help (that didn't cost her budget anything) would be welcome. As it turned out, though, it was the nuns that were looking for help.

They were looking for something else, as well.

The pale nun led Mrs Gribbins to Sister Helena. She was in the Great Hall, a large vaulted room strung with tapestries. She was a tall woman who seemed to be made even taller by the black habit. She had perfect ivory flesh that made Mrs Gribbins think that even some nuns followed a skin care regime. On the other hand, perhaps Sister Helena was just lucky. Either way, she had the kind of face you expected to find on the cover of a magazine, not under a wimple.

The news Mrs Gribbins brought for Sister Helena, however, wasn't going to put a smile on that cover-girl face.

'You're sure it was the talisman?' Sister Helena demanded, when Mrs Gribbins had finished telling her about the reporter Sarah Jane Smith's visit, and what she had seen through the bird-watching binoculars.

'Absolutely,' said Mrs Gribbins. 'I saw her give it to the boy.'

Sister Helena strode across the room, the fabric of her habit flapping angrily around her. An angry nun was something Mrs Gribbins had thought she would never see. But then, nuns that paid her handsomely to sneak into the rest home by night and search the residents' belongings was something she never expected to come across, either.

'Why would she give the talisman to the boy

unless she knew we were looking for it?' Sister Helena growled. 'You told us she barely knows her own name.'

Mrs Gribbins noticed that her hands were shaking. Whoever these nuns really were, she knew they were about something much darker than singing hymns. The thought of antagonizing one of them really didn't seem like a good idea.

From her pocket, Mrs Gribbins pulled the business card that the journalist had given her and tried to soothe Sister Helena's rage. 'I know where you can find the boy,' she said.

Sister Helena snatched the card and glanced at it, as she walked away and tugged on a bell pull. She didn't seem any happier.

'We've paid you well for your assistance, Mrs Gribbins, but this complicates everything.'

Mrs Gribbins wanted to justify herself to Sister Helena she knew she had been well paid. But she had done everything they had asked of her, and when she had finally realized where the Nelson-Stanley woman had hidden the jewel that her husband had once stolen from their order, she had come straight to the abbey to tell them. But before she could say a word, the double doors at the end of the Great Hall opened and two nuns advanced through it. Mrs Gribbins knew they were coming for her. And that sent a chill down her spine.

'The Abbess will want to see you,' said Sister Helena. She turned her back on Mrs Gribbins and left the room.

Mrs Gribbins saw no alternative but to go with the two nuns that stood, silent, waiting for her. They walked either side of her, leading her through the abbey. They didn't speak. They barely looked at her. Mrs Gribbins fought the chill anxiety that she felt creeping through her body. For goodness' sake, they were *nuns*, she tried to tell herself, what were they going to do to her? The Abbess was probably some shrunken old biddy with a walking stick that was going to try to give her a telling off for slipping up like this. Well, Sylvia Gribbins dealt with people just like that on a day-to-day basis. She would tell the Abbess exactly what she told the odd disgruntled resident at Lavender Lawns: they got value for money but sometimes things – like the community room TV blowing up half an hour before the latest *Corrie* wedding – were just beyond her control.

The thought made her smile. She could deal with the Abbess.

And then the nuns came to a door and knocked. They waited a moment, then opened it and stood back. Neither of them made any movement to enter, they just stood there and waited for Mrs Gribbins to step over the threshold.

She was psyched up now, and ready to give the old Abbess as good as she got. Mrs Gribbins stepped into the room, and the door closed behind her.

It was a small room, with no furniture except a simple bed and chair. In the chair sat a dark shape. As her eyes fell on it, all the confidence that she had mustered on the way there seemed to soak into the cold flagstones beneath her feet.

The dark shape was a nun. Small, thin and old. Very old, from the look of her hands. The nun was veiled; Mrs Gribbins couldn't see her face. All she could see of her were her hands – dark, shrivelled hands, with skin that looked more like tree bark than living flesh. But it was the nails that made Mrs Gribbins shudder. Her fingernails were long and twisted, uncut in decades, like hideous talons.

The Abbess didn't move, but Mrs Gribbins knew she was watching her through the dark veil that hid her face.

Mrs Gribbins' mouth had gone dry; she tried to speak...

Then the Abbess's hands moved to her veil, and raised it.

And Mrs Gribbins screamed.

Chapter Five

Bea

A t about the time that Sylvia Gribbins was striking the door of St Agnes' Abbey, Sarah Jane Smith stood in the middle of her attic, that she used as an office and centre of operations when alien-hunting, and called out.

'Mr Smith, I need you.'

Bricks in the wall broke apart and clouds of steam burst out of the opening that yawned wider as hidden hydraulics thundered into action somewhere behind the attic brickwork. The computer that Sarah Jane called Mr Smith emerged from the wall.

Clyde, who stood a little behind Sarah Jane in the attic, always loved to see Mr Smith coming out of the wall.

Awesome!

He thought the same thing every time it happened.

He also kind of wondered what had made Sarah Jane call the computer *Mr Smith*. There was something about Sarah Jane, he thought, that was a little bit sad.

Mr Smith spoke, 'Yes, Sarah Jane. What can I do for you?'

'The Lavender Lawns Rest Home is apparently being haunted by a nun. I need you to access the central land registry database and see if there is anything to historically support the possibility.'

'Of a haunting?'

Clyde thought it sounded like Mr Smith was taking the Mickey. He liked that. Mr Smith had some attitude.

Sarah Jane told the computer to just run the check.

Clyde glanced around for Luke. He'd been right behind him when they'd come up to the attic, now he'd slunk off to the other end of the room. He was sitting in a chair with his back to them, and seemed to be looking at something. Clyde was about to check out what he was up to, but then Mr Smith was talking again...

'There is no record of any past ecclesiastical building on the site of Lavender Lawns.'

'So no obvious reason for the home to be haunted by a nun, then?' said Sarah Jane.

'I assume that by haunting you mean the projection of energies imprinted on psychic-assimilating matter,' observed Mr Smith.

'Obviously,' she said. Like it was a stupid question.

'Come again?' Clyde pleaded.

Sarah Jane glanced at him, a little impatient, 'Events get recorded on their surroundings then, under certain circumstances get played back.'

'Like video?'

Sarah Jane smiled. Clyde liked to play the joker, but he was far from stupid. 'Exactly,' she said.

'Sarah Jane.' Mr Smith was talking again, 'Are you aware that Luke has brought an unidentified element of alien technology into the attic?'

Sarah Jane and Clyde whirled around to look at Luke. He couldn't have hidden the talisman that he had been secretly studying, had he tried. It glowed with an eerie green light.

'Whoah!' said Clyde. 'No way did that come off the Shopping Channel!'

Sarah Jane held out her hand.

'Give it to me, Luke,' she said, as if he might have been holding the wrong end of a snake.

Luke passed the glowing talisman to Sarah Jane and explained anxiously, 'One of the residents gave it to me. Mrs Nelson-Stanley. She said someone was looking for it, but they mustn't find it. And I had to keep it a secret. Sorry. Was that wrong?'

'I'm not sure,' said Sarah Jane. She was studying the talisman, its light bathing her face in its weird glow. 'Mr Smith, is it safe?'

Mr Smith, who Clyde now reckoned could also be a bit of a telltale as well as having attitude, said, 'Insufficient data. I'd like to carry out a detailed analysis.'

A tray emerged from Mr Smith, like a hand asking for the talisman. Sarah Jane was placing the object on it when Maria came through the attic door and slammed it shut after her.

Sarah Jane spun around, angry, 'Do you mind? There's a lot of sensitive equipment in here!'

Moist-eyed, Maria said she was sorry, and Sarah Jane saw that she had been crying and felt sorry, too.

'What's going on?' Maria asked, determined

that no one was going to notice she was upset.

Clyde filled her in, 'Some old biddy's given Luke an alien gizmo!'

He pointed Maria to the talisman just before Mr Smith took it and began his analysis.

Luke was feeling confused. He had tried to keep Mrs Nelson-Stanley's promise, but at the same time he knew he should have said something to Sarah Jane straight away.

'Mrs Nelson-Stanley said the nun at Lavender Lawns wasn't a ghost – and it's looking for the talisman.'

Sarah Jane was going to have to talk to Mrs Nelson-Stanley. Where did an old lady in a rest home get an alien stone like that? Its setting and the chain on it suggested someone had worn it as a pendant. Why was she hiding it from a nun? Sarah Jane felt the questions piling up, and with them came the thrill that had never faded in all these years – the thrill of something extra-terrestrial.

She turned to Maria. Did she want to come with her?

Maria nodded.

'You two stay here,' Sarah Jane told the boys. It wasn't a punishment, but if Maria wanted to talk during the drive to Lavender Lawns she might find it easier without Luke and Clyde there. But they took it like a punishment, all the same. Luke complained that Mrs Nelson-Stanley had entrusted the talisman to him, and Clyde reckoned that it was he who had brought Sarah Jane in on it.

'It's – like – my case,' he said.

But Sarah Jane wasn't debating. She told them to stay put and swept out of there with Maria.

As they pulled out of the drive and headed up Bannerman Road, Sarah Jane saw Maria cast a glance at her own house.

'Mum's back,' she said.

'Oh,' said Sarah Jane.

'Just for a few days. Not permanently, or anything.'

'I see.' Sarah Jane didn't need to ask how Maria felt about that, it was as clear as the red rings around her eyes, a little confused, and more than a little angry.

She gave Maria time to talk if she wanted to. Sarah Jane wanted to help if she could, to be a shoulder to cry on if that's what Maria needed. But Maria's feelings and how she felt about the mother that had walked out on her were hers to share, not for Sarah Jane to probe. Maria didn't talk about her mum after that, she asked about Lavender Lawns, and on the way Sarah Jane gave her a run-down on what had taken her there that morning.

When they reached the rest home, Edith Randall was sitting in a deckchair on the lawn. She was surprised and delighted to see Sarah Jane back so soon and wondered if Maria was the photographer – everyone seemed to be so young these days, she said. Sarah Jane explained that she had returned to see Mrs Nelson-Stanley.

Edith shook her head sorrowfully. 'You won't get any sense out of her, Miss Smith. It's the Alzheimer's, you know.'

'Oh,' said Sarah Jane. That was something she hadn't expected. There was a good chance Mrs Nelson-Stanley wouldn't be able to remember how she came by the talisman. On the other hand, she had seemed pretty convinced that someone was trying to take it from her. That could have been down to her mental condition, of course.

Edith took Sarah Jane and Maria up to Bea Nelson-Stanley's room. She knocked, and when there was no answer, Edith opened the door and led the others in.

'She won't have gone far, I'm sure,' said Edith.

Sarah Jane and Maria were taking in the room. Bea Nelson-Stanley didn't collect Toby jugs like her neighbour, she collected (or had collected in her younger days) marvellous things from all around the world. Ancient jade Chinese figures, an Egyptian burial scarab, tribal masks and totems...Sarah Jane gasped with the joy of it. Bea's room was like a small museum.

Edith recognized her awe and smiled sadly, 'Yes, it's such a tragedy, isn't it? Struck down by that disease after the life she must have led.'

'She's been everywhere,' Maria said, her eyes scanning the photographs that hung among the trophies of her travels. There was a young woman in many of them, tall, lean and very attractive. The pictures were mostly black and white. Maria thought the woman – she guessed it was Bea Nelson-Stanley – was dressed for the 1950s. The pictures were all taken in exotic locations. Maria could identify the Pyramids, of course, and another seemed to be in the ruins of what looked like an Aztec temple. Beside her in some of the photographs was a broad-chested, bronzed man.

'Was that her husband?' Maria asked.

'Yes. He was an archaeologist,' Edith said.

'They went all over the world together.'

Maria indicated the walls, 'No kidding?'

'He died five years ago. Poor Bea started to lose it after that, and that's when she washed up here.'

'Does anybody visit her?' asked Sarah Jane.

Edith shook her head, 'No children. Too busy having adventures, from the look of it. All well and good, but adventures don't look after you when you're old, do they?'

No, Sarah Jane supposed, they didn't, and she tried not to think about how things would be when she was Bea's age.

Then Maria saw something in one of the photographs.

'That's the talisman!'

Sarah Jane looked. In the picture, Bea's archaeologist husband had an arm around her shoulders, and around her neck hung the amulet that Luke had brought into the attic.

Edith was puzzled – what talisman? She had thought they were there to talk to Bea about the ghost. And then Bea came through the door, examining the strangers in her room with blue eyes that – despite her age and the condition of her mind – still shone like those of a girl.

'You've got visitors, Bea,' Edith explained.

Bea took in Sarah Jane and Maria, 'Do I know you? I'm sorry, but these days I'm not very good with faces.'

Sarah Jane introduced herself and Maria, and Edith told Bea that Sarah Jane was a reporter.

'Oh,' said Bea. 'It's my husband you want to talk to, then.'

Edith gave Sarah Jane a look – *I warned you.* And Sarah Jane's heart melted for Bea.

'It's you I came to talk to,' she said gently, and indicated the talisman in the old photograph. 'Can you tell me where you got this talisman?'

Bea smiled, and stroked the photograph. Sarah Jane saw her eyes moisten as her long fingers traced the shape of her dead husband on the yellowing picture.

'That's Edgar,' she said. 'My husband.'

Sarah Jane and Maria looked at each other. Bea had loved her husband very much, and if in her confusion sometimes she still thought he was alive, perhaps that wasn't such a bad thing.

'He always said the Sontarans were quite the silliest-looking race in the galaxy.'

Sarah Jane felt the colour slip out of her face. She stared at Bea and had to struggle to find her

Sarah Jane shows Bea that the sonic lipstick and the talisman are both alien artefacts.

Clyde and Maria sneak into the abbey trying to find Luke.

The Gorgon's face is revealed and...

...Maria's father is turned to stone.

Maria is panic stricken by what her father has become.

Luke and Clyde emerge from the secret tunnels of the abbey.

Sister Helena brandishes the talisman she has recovered from Sarah Jane.

Maria pleads with Bea to give her some information to save her Dad.

When Luke and Clyde escape with the talisman, the nuns surround them.

Sarah Jane is brought before the Gorgon.

The Gorgon points to her new host – Sarah Jane.

Sarah Jane struggles to escape from the nuns.

Sister Helena prepares to lift the Gorgon's veil.

The Gorgon is destroyed.

Maria hugs Sarah Jane and apologises for being at angry with her.

Sarah Jane and Maria return the talisman to Bea.

voice, 'What did you say?'

Edith shook her head, 'Oh, she's always talking rubbish about spacemen and monsters.'

Sarah Jane felt her mind reeling with shock. She had encountered Sontarans twice when she travelled with the Doctor – that was the man that had taken her on incredible journeys through time and space. Although, in a way, both encounters had been with different Doctors. Sometimes he changed. But that was something you had to get used to if you travelled with the Doctor. She had met him again many years after their journeys and adventures together had come to an end. He had changed again. Yet hadn't changed at all.

And then Sarah Jane found herself smiling, and almost reached out and hugged Bea. 'She's seen Sontarans,' she gasped, amazed and delighted.

Maria looked lost. 'What's a Sontaran?'

Bea gave Maria her answer, 'The silliest-looking race in the galaxy! That's what Edgar used to say. Like a great big potato with a – a – ray gun!' Bea waved her walking cane for emphasis. 'Quite nasty blighters they were, all the same.'

'Oh, yes, Bea, they are!' Sarah Jane laughed. 'You're absolutely right!'

Edith clucked with disapproval, 'It's no good

encouraging her, Miss Smith. She'll just go on and on about monsters.'

I don't mind if she does, Sarah Jane thought to herself. *If she has seen Sontarans, then maybe she has seen so much more.*

But, of course, Edith put all Bea's talk of monsters down to the Alzheimer's eating away at her mind, making her confuse reality with old films that maybe she had once seen with Edgar.

'The Gorgon,' said Edith, 'She's always on about that one. I saw it at the flicks years ago. Christopher Lee and Barbara Shelley with all snakes for hair. Bonkers.'

Chapter Six

Weirdo nuns

L uke got the door.

When Sarah Jane took off with Maria and left them in the attic, Clyde had blamed Luke. According to Clyde, he should have told Sarah Jane about the talisman, straight away. What had Luke been thinking? Didn't the weird glow tell him it was alien and important? Luke told him he knew that, but he had made a promise. Promises were one thing, Clyde argued, but remembering who your friends were – that came first! Luke now felt awful. And Clyde saw the hurt in his friend's eyes and felt bad about having a go – he sometimes forgot that Luke might have looked fourteen, but had really only been around a few months. That superbrain of his had helped him catch up a lot, but there was still a long way to go. There were some things that being ultra-intelligent couldn't help you with– little things like relationships, and bigger stuff like being funny and cool. Clyde had made himself kind of Luke's lifecoach to help him sort things out. He made a mental note to sort out the ground rules on making and keeping promises and pass them on to Luke.

By way of making up, they took each other on at *Alien Devastation 3*, and as Luke blasted ugly alien invaders apart Clyde told him he was letting him win.

Then the doorbell went, and Luke went to get it.

He found a nun on the doorstep.

'Hello,' she beamed. She had perfect alabaster skin and the kind of smile that sold tooth whitener by the bucket-load. 'I'm Sister Helena from St Agnes's Abbey.'

Luke sensed Clyde coming into the hall behind him and felt grateful. What you did when an old lady entrusted an alien talisman to you in the morning so that some mysterious nun didn't get her hands on it, then a nun turned up on your doorstep in the afternoon – that was one of those situations that Luke wasn't all that clear on.

'Who might you be?' asked Sister Helena, still all smiles.

'He's Luke. I'm Clyde.'

Sister Helena took that in with a simple blink of her emerald green eyes. Clyde found himself wondering if she was blonde under that cowl on her head, then felt vaguely worried about fancying a nun.

'And which one of you two fine young men was at Lavender Lawns today and left with a gift from one of the old ladies?'

Maybe she reminded Clyde just a little bit of Claudia Schiffer, but she also made him think of big red emergency lights and sirens whooping out a very loud danger signal.

'Don't know what you're talking about,' he said.

Then Luke just had to say something, didn't he?

'How would you know if she gave me anything, any way? She wouldn't have told you.'

'Can it, Luke,' Clyde hissed.

But Luke was probably the kind of kid that

would prod a sleeping tiger just to see if it was as dangerous as people said.

'Why have you been hunting through the old people's rooms looking for the talisman?'

'Luke!' Clyde exploded, and started to push the door shut. 'Okay, that's enough! See you, Sister!'

But Sister Helena moved fast. She had her foot in the door before Clyde could close it.

'Boys,' she said, 'you don't know what you've got your hands on!'

She said it like she was worried about them. But Clyde didn't buy that for a second.

'Well, you're not getting your hands on it, either,' he told her, and tried to slam the door – nun's foot or no foot.

But Sister Helena wasn't going anywhere – although the smile had gone, and so had any attempt to fool the boys that she was worried about them.

'Give me that talisman,' she snarled.

That was when Alan Jackson showed up, 'Hello, Sister. Collection, is it?'

Sister Helena turned around, bemused, to see Maria's dad standing there, hands in his jeans pockets, an easy smile on his face.

'Abbey roofs don't fix themselves,' she said after a moment. She flashed that smile again and Clyde could see Alan wondering about the colour of her hair under the wimple, too. 'That's one miracle we're still waiting on.'

Alan dug some money out his jeans, a fiver and a couple of pound coins. 'Well, I always give to needy causes. You could say it's a good *habit* of mine,' he grinned.

Sister Helena looked at him, then forced a giggle at the lame joke. She ignored the offered couple of quid and took the fiver. Sparing the two boys a brief, blistering look, she moved off down the drive. Alan watched her go, and Luke and Clyde relaxed, then he turned back to them and asked if they had seen Maria.

'She was a bit upset earlier,' he explained.

And she wasn't the only one. He'd had a massive row with Chrissie since Maria had stormed out. A lot of old wounds had been opened.

'She's gone out with Sarah Jane,' Luke told him.

'Look, do me a favour, will you?' Alan asked, clearly worried – he didn't like the way things had been left with his daughter. 'When they get back, tell her I was looking for her. Please.'

Luke told him that they would, and Alan smiled his grateful thanks and left.

Clyde figured that then was as good as any time to give Luke his next lesson in 'Getting By on Planet Earth for Those Who Haven't Got A Clue'...

'Listen, when weirdo nuns turn up on your doorstep, asking you about freaky glowing alien gizmos, one thing you never do – all right? – is tell them that you've got one. Okay?'

Luke looked at him, blankly. 'I didn't,' he said.

'Good as,' said Clyde.

'Look, we should call Mum and tell her what's happened.'

Clyde nodded and took out his mobile. That, at least, was a good idea. He started thumbing through for Sarah Jane's number, then stopped. He had a better idea.

'Better still,' he said, 'we should get round there, and tell her.'

'Isn't phoning quicker?'

Clyde's eyes glittered, 'Sure, we could phone. Or we could get round to Lavender Lawns and get back in on the action. Yeah?'

Luke didn't need to be super intelligent to see

the sense in that.

As they set off to the bus stop, they didn't see the big old hearse parked around the corner from Bannerman Road, or Sister Helena who was sitting in the back seat watching them.

Chapter Seven

Long-gone adventures

Edith Randall had left Sarah Jane and Maria to it with Bea. She didn't understand all this talk about a talisman, and it became clear that no one was going to tell her. And if Sarah Jane and her young friend expected Bea to tell them anything about it – anything that made any sense, at least – well, they were going to be in for a very long wait. Edith had better things to do with her time.

And Bea hadn't really said much for a while. Sarah Jane and Maria sat there and Bea hummed to herself. Sarah Jane recognized the song, *Slow Boat to China*.

'So, if Bea had this talisman, and it's alien, and she's seen these Sontarans, then she isn't just talking about a bunch of old horror movies, like Mrs Randall thinks, is she?'

Sarah Jane looked at Maria, then back to Bea, 'Aliens have been coming to Earth for centuries, Maria. Maybe Bea's adventures with her archaeologist husband involved a lot more than just old pots and bones.'

'*I'd love to get you on a slow boat to China,*' Bea sang. Then she looked at Sarah Jane for the first time in ages, 'That was our song. Edgar had such a lovely voice.'

Sarah Jane smiled, 'Did he? I'm sure he was quite a man.'

But Bea had begun humming to herself again, once more lost in her own world. Sarah Jane ached to be let in there.

'It's so sad,' Maria said. 'The things she must have seen. And now everyone thinks she's crazy.'

Sarah Jane looked around the room, a room filled with memories of long-gone adventures, and loneliness.

'Who knows where any of us will end up?' she said.

Sarah Jane reached out and laid her hand over

Bea's. 'But someone doesn't think you're crazy, do they, Bea? Someone knows what that talisman is, and they want it.'

Abruptly, Bea stopped humming and fixed her eyes on Sarah Jane, 'The talisman?'

A thrill of excitement shot through Sarah Jane. 'Yes, Bea! The talisman. Tell me what you know. I promise I'll believe you. Sometimes people have thought I've been mad, but I've seen things, too. Just like you!'

Bea's eyes floated towards the window, her mind floating back decades...

'Edgar unearthed it at a dig in...' She screwed up her face with the effort of pulling the word from her damaged brain...'In Syria.'

The memory made her smile, 'He gave it to me.'

She savoured the special memory for a few seconds, then her smile faded, 'Of course, he had no idea what it was. Had no idea.'

'So what was it?' asked Maria.

And Bea's fingers suddenly gripped the arms of her chair, her eyes blazed with terror. 'They mustn't find it! They mustn't!'

Sarah Jane reached out to her again, tried to comfort her, 'Who, Bea? Who do you mean?'

'The Sisters!'

'You mean, as in nuns?' asked Maria.

'They protect her!'

'Protect who?' asked Sarah Jane.

Bea fought hard for the word, but this time it wasn't just down to the Alzheimer's. She was scared to speak it.

'Who?' Sarah Jane urged. 'Who are they protecting? Who wants the talisman?'

Bea forced its name out, 'The Gorgon!'

Chapter Eight

Kidnapped

As the big black hearse slid alongside them on the road, Clyde figured the best thing to do was to just keep on walking.

'Come on,' he said, 'it's Sister Sinister again.'

As he spoke the nun was already getting out of the hearse. She was going for the sweet, concerned nun approach again. 'Don't run away, Luke. I won't hurt you. I just want us to have a little talk.'

Yeah, thought Clyde, *and you'll tell us all about raindrops on roses and whiskers on kittens!*

'Don't listen to her, Luke. No way is she really a nun,' he warned, backing off from Sister Helena. Two other nuns had now also slipped out of the hearse.

Oh, brother! Hench-nuns!

Sister Helena broadened that toothpaste smile and opened her arms. 'Whatever else would I be, but a nun?' she asked.

'I don't know,' Clyde told her. 'But I bet you ain't got legs under them robes, just a bench of slimy tentacles or something.' He noted with relief that he was way past fancying her now.

Sister Helena laughed. 'Your friend watches too much TV, Luke. I think perhaps we could talk a little more sensibly without him. Jump in the car and we'll go to the abbey.'

Luke shook his head, 'I don't think so.'

'You're safe with me,' she said.

'We're not going anywhere with you,' Clyde told her.

'It's not an open invitation,' she scowled. Then she turned back to Luke, 'Listen to your friend here and you'll be in far more danger, I guarantee. But I can help you. I want to help you.'

'The talisman is dangerous?' Luke asked.

'More than you can possibly imagine.'

And Clyde could see Luke looking inside the hearse, thinking about getting in. Clyde was about to speak up, to tell him not to be an idiot – but Sister Helena had already seen her chance, her hand was in the small of Luke's back and before either of them knew it, Luke was in the big black car.

Clyde leaped forward. 'No!'

But Sister Helena turned on him, and Clyde didn't quite know what happened next. He felt the slightest pressure of her hand on his chest and then he was on his back on the pavement and the hearse was pulling away from the kerb – Luke trapped inside.

Clyde rolled to his feet and pulled his mobile from his pocket. He was thumbing up Sarah Jane's number as he ran.

Meanwhile, Sarah Jane and Maria were walking across Lavender Lawns' gravel drive towards the little blue car. Bea's outburst about the Gorgon had been the last thing she had said. No matter how much Sarah Jane tried, the old lady wouldn't talk, just sat in her chair singing to herself. Whatever had happened to her in the past, whatever sort of encounter that talisman had brought about, it had clearly been terrifying.

But a Gorgon?

'It's Greek mythology, right?' said Maria.

Sarah Jane remembered the story, 'There were three, *The Daughters of Phorcys the Sea God and*

Ceto. Medusa, Stheno and Euryale.'

'All snakes for hair and turning people to stone just by looking at them?' Maria was having a hard time believing that.

And that was when Sarah Jane's phone went. 'Hello?'

On the other end of the line, Clyde was gasping for breath as he ran, 'Luke – he's been nabbed by a nun!'

'He's been what?! How?'

Clyde quickly outlined what had happened. Sarah Jane asked where he was and told him to stay there – she was coming to get him. Snapping the phone shut, she told Maria to get into the car and gunned its engine. Gravel flew as it pulled away. Fifteen minutes later she found Clyde at the side of the road. He told her that Sister Helena had mentioned St Agnes's Abbey and another fifteen minutes later Sarah Jane was pulling up outside it.

Sarah Jane wasn't big on plans. Experience had taught her that too much could go wrong with a plan; it always relied on other people and other things doing what you expected them to. Aliens rarely did what you expected them to do, so Sarah Jane didn't waste time formulating plans.

But she had a quick brain. She could think on her feet. She relied on that. And, if it came to it, she could still use them to run pretty fast, too. But as she hammered on the abbey door she had a *bit* of a plan and as she glanced over her shoulder at the little blue car she was satisfied that it looked, from here, as if it was empty.

A nun opened the door to Sarah Jane, who pushed a Press card in her face. It was fake, one of several that she sometimes used.

'Hello. My name's Felicity Barnes. I'm doing a story for *The Times* on religion in the twenty-first Century. Is there anyone I can talk to?'

The nun looked doubtful.

'Perhaps Sister Helena?' Sarah Jane suggested and, as she had hoped, the name got her inside.

Clyde and Maria, crouched down in the little blue Nissan, counted to a hundred then crept out, still keeping low. With the car between them and the abbey, they checked the coast was clear then made a dash for the building. Sarah Jane had used Sister Helena's name – they were going to have to find an unlocked door, or an open window.

It took them a few minutes, but they eventually found what they were looking for – a window at the side of the abbey that had been opened just a few inches to let the summer air inside. Clyde got it open all the way and the two of them climbed in.

They found themselves in a bare passageway with a wooden floor that creaked with every step, no matter how carefully they trod.

'Now what?' Clyde whispered. 'Where do we go?'

'I don't know,' Maria told him – *like she would have a clue!* 'What do nuns generally do with the kids they kidnap?'

Okay, Clyde considered himself told. And when they came to the first door in the passageway, it seemed to Maria like as good a place to start as any. She reached for the handle – and found Clyde wrapping his own hand around hers.

'Hold on. What if it's in there? This Gorgon.'

Maria looked at him, despairing. 'Then just keep your eyes closed and hold my hand.'

Yeah, like he was going to do that! Clyde Langer wasn't chicken. And just to prove it, he opened the door and went in first.

They found themselves in a small room, empty but for a simple bed and a chair – and a woman that Clyde immediately recognized from

Lavender Lawns... Mrs Gribbins stood there, her face contorted with horror, and her body turned to stone!

As one, Clyde and Maria turned to get out of there – and found the doorway blocked by a dark shape, its face veiled, its hands like claws.

Chapter Nine

No choice

Sarah Jane leafed through a large, old book. She was surrounded by books. The nun who had opened the abbey door had led her into the library and locked her in.

So much for fake ID, Sarah Jane thought. But she wasn't too concerned. As long as no harm had come to Luke. And she didn't imagine that it would be long before Sister Helena showed up and she started to get to the bottom of things.

In the meantime she had taken a look around the library, and among the books there was an elaborate volume on Greek Mythology. In it she found a beautifully detailed illustration of Perseus slaying the Gorgon, Medusa.

The ancient story went that Perseus set out on a quest to kill Medusa and bring back her head as a wedding gift for King Polydectes, who was forcing Perseus's mother to marry him. Armed with gifts from the gods – a magical sword and a highly polished bronze shield – Perseus set out to hunt down the dreaded Gorgons. He found them sleeping in a cave, and by viewing the three ghastly sisters only by the reflection in his mirror-like shield, was able to cut off Medusa's head without being turned to stone by the sight of her, and escape before the surviving sisters caught him. Perseus sailed home with Medusa's head in a bag and presented it to Polydectes as he prepared for the wedding. But as soon as Polydectes set eyes on the decapitated Gorgon's head it turned him to stone.

That was the story. But Sarah Jane knew well that some legends were more than just ancient soap opera. They didn't have newspapers and twenty-four-hour TV news to flash events around the Ancient World. The news anchormen of ancient Greece were poets like Homer, who heard stories and wrote them down. Who knew the origins of those stories? But sometimes, just sometimes – Sarah Jane knew – when there was a monster involved in them there was every chance that someone had encountered a creature from another world.

The sound of the library door being unlocked roused Sarah Jane from her thoughts. A moment later Luke was in the room. Sarah Jane flung her arms around him.

'Luke! Are you all right?'

He seemed a little bemused by the question. He told her he was fine.

And Sarah Jane's relief gave way to anger, 'What do you think you were doing, getting into a stranger's car? For an intelligent boy, sometimes I can't believe how stupid you are!'

He started to protest that he hadn't just got into the car, but they both heard the whispering rustle of Sister Helena's habit as she joined them in the library.

'Luke was never in any danger, Miss Smith. But it seemed that bringing him to the abbey was the fastest way of attracting your attention. Although your two other young friends were a surprise.'

As she spoke, Maria and Clyde ran into the room. Behind them came two more nuns, followed by the Abbess.

'We found Mrs Gribbins,' gasped Clyde.

'She's been turned to stone,' said Maria.

Sister Helena looked genuinely regretful, 'Unfortunately, Mrs Gribbins always was something of an old fossil.'

Sarah Jane gathered the kids behind her, 'Is it true, then? Are you really protecting a Gorgon here?'

One corner of Sister Helena's mouth lifted and her eyes glittered as if someone had said something funny. 'A creature with writhing serpents for hair?' she asked, looking at the book Sarah Jane had just put down. 'Those melodramatic Greeks. They never could resist embellishing a story.'

She closed the heavy book with a thump, and turned back to face Sarah Jane. The smile had gone. 'As you've heard, however, the myth isn't entirely without foundation.'

Maria was determined that the nun wasn't going to think she was in the least bit scared. 'But it's an alien, right?'

Sister Helena's gaze fell on the Abbess as she spoke, 'The Gorgons travelled to our world 3,000 years ago. Once there were three. Now only one.'

And Sarah Jane knew it was standing there in the room with them, its face covered by a black veil.

'Generations of our sisterhood have served

and protected the Gorgons down the centuries,' said Sister Helena, and Sarah Jane could see something like love in the nun's eyes when she looked at the creature in the veil. Sarah Jane felt her blood run cold.

'What happened to the other two?' she asked.

'One was killed in the ancient days, when our sisterhood still served Demeter, when the key was stolen.'

And that was when Sarah Jane saw it all. 'The key to whatever brought the Gorgons to Earth,' she said. 'And the Sisters have been searching for it ever since. Did you get close once, Sister Helena? Maybe fifty years ago? Was that when the second Gorgon died?'

Sister Helena scowled, 'Professor Nelson-Stanley and his meddlesome wife!' She moved closer to Sarah Jane, her features softened. 'But you have the key now, Miss Smith. I'm sure you will be more reasonable.'

Sarah Jane told her not to bet on it. Kidnapping and turning people to stone didn't bring out the best in her.

Sister Helena became almost pleading. 'The Gorgon is old. The talisman opens a portal to the Gorgon world. She only wants to go home to die.

You can understand that, can't you? Would you deny her?'

Sarah Jane looked from Sister Helena to the silent, shrouded creature, then back at Luke and the others.

'Why should I believe you?' she asked.

Sister Helena's voice was quiet. Sarah Jane imagined she might even pray in that voice. She said, 'You have no choice.'

Sarah Jane took in the room, the nuns, the kids and the creature that stood there in a veil that covered things that she didn't want to think about. One thing was for sure – she had to get Luke, Clyde and Maria out of there.

'All right,' she said. 'We'll get it.'

But Sister Helena wasn't stupid. 'The two boys will stay here.'

Sarah Jane tried to argue, but she knew that Sister Helena was holding the high cards. Luke and Clyde would be safe, as long as Sarah Jane didn't try to trick them – which Sarah Jane knew was exactly what she had to do. The question was, how? She didn't buy Sister Helena's story that the Gorgon only wanted to go home. Not for a second. So there was no way that she could hand over the talisman. But how could she not do that, and get the boys back safe and sound? As she drove back to Bannerman Road with Maria, Sister Helena and the Abbess following in the hearse, Sarah Jane went over the situation in her head again and again, searching for a way out.

When they reached the house, the nuns followed Sarah Jane and Maria inside. Sarah Jane told them she was going upstairs to get the talisman, Sister Helena closed a hand over Maria's shoulder and said that she would stay there with them.

Maria watched Sarah Jane go upstairs, then turned to look at the Abbess. She hadn't made a sound all this time.

'Doesn't she speak English?' Maria asked Sister Helena.

'The Gorgon doesn't need to speak.'

'You mean she's – like – telepathic? Is that how she controls you?' Maria grinned, still determined not to show how afraid she felt, 'I mean, looking after a Gorgon isn't exactly normal for a bunch of nuns, is it?'

The Abbess turned towards Maria. Despite the black veil, Maria could feel the creature's eyes on her.

Sister Helena whispered in her ear, 'I'd shut

up, if I were you, or the Abbess might show you her idea of solving a problem like Maria.'

It was advice from a sinister nun who served a 3,000 year-old monster that could turn people to stone. It seemed worth taking. And then Maria heard Sarah Jane coming down the stairs, she saw the talisman in one hand – and noted that the other was hidden. Sister Helena didn't notice that, her eyes were on the talisman.

'The key to the portal!'

As Sister Helena made a move to take it, Sarah Jane stepped back and revealed the sonic lipstick in her other hand. She pointed it directly at the talisman and the sonic lipstick emitted a low warbling sound.

'Either you let my son and his friend go, or I'll destroy the talisman with sonic disruption!'

But Sister Helena only shook her head sorrowfully, 'I warned you, Miss Smith. Now look on the face of the Gorgon and feel your flesh turn to stone!'

And the Abbess's claw-like hands moved to the veil.

Sarah Jane pulled Maria to her, 'Don't look, Maria!'

And no one heard the unlocked front door

open, or the footsteps in the hall.

Alan was walking in on them before anyone knew he was there.

'Hello? The door was...'

And his eyes fell on the face of the Gorgon.

'Dad!' Maria screamed. 'Don't look at it!'

It wasn't an alien face – not quite. It looked like the face of an incredibly old woman, shrunken, creased and leathery. Her eyes were blank and staring. Her mouth, lined with ragged and rotten teeth, fell open, and from it came a hideous cry. And with the cry – a terrible noise of fury and pain – came the snakes, thrashing, serpentine beams of cold blue light that leaped from between her jaws and burst from her blank eyes and surged across the room, engulfing Alan.

It took a couple of heartbeats.

Then Alan's heart beat no more.

He stood there, a statue of cold, dead stone!

Chapter Ten

Escape

'Dad!' Maria screamed it like her heart would burst.

Sarah Jane held her tight, tried to cover her eyes, 'Don't look, Maria!'

But it was no good. She had seen what her father had become. He stood in Sarah Jane's lounge, flesh turned to stone. A statue.

In the confusion and panic Sister Helena had grabbed the talisman. She now held it, triumphant, as the Abbess drew down her veil again. Sister Helena turned to look at Sarah Jane, 'Pay heed to the Gorgon's warning, and don't interfere.'

She raised the talisman high and spoke to the Abbess, 'After 3,000 years, the doorway to your people can be opened again!'

'And then what?' asked Sarah Jane as she cradled weeping Maria in her arms. 'Invasion?'

Sister Helena turned on Sarah Jane, scornful. 'The Gorgons need us to survive, Miss Smith. Opening the portal to their world isn't opening the door to invasion, but salvation!'

'You're mad!' Sarah Jane spat.

Sister Helena's face froze. 'Remember – don't interfere!'

And, with the Abbess, she swept out of the house.

Maria broke away from Sarah Jane and reached out towards what had, until seconds ago been her father. her fingers brushed the stone hand that had held her only a couple of hours before as he tried to comfort her. Now it was hard and cold. And Maria felt a wave of guilt crash over her – if only she hadn't run out on him like that...if only she hadn't argued with her mum...'I didn't mean to shout at you, Dad. I'm sorry...I'm so sorry.'

Maria sobbed, felt her heart shattering inside her chest. Her Dad was dead. Turned to stone. And it was all her fault!

She felt Sarah Jane take her by the shoulders and turn her around to face her. 'Listen to me,' she said, looking straight into Maria's eyes.

'Listen to me. You are not going to fall apart. Do you understand me? Whatever has happened to your father, there's one thing I've learned after all these years – there is *always* a chance. Do you hear me?'

But Maria didn't hear. She was overwhelmed by a tide of grief and guilt. She was drowning in it.

'Mum was right!' she gasped. 'I should never have had anything to do with you! It's all your fault!'

Sarah Jane felt it like a slap in the face.

'You and your aliens! I wish I'd never seen that one in your garden! I wish I'd never seen you! Everything was fine 'til we moved here!'

Then, sobbing, she collapsed into Sarah Jane's arms, but the truth of what Maria said burned Sarah Jane like drops of acid on her skin. She had warned Maria when it all began, of course she had. She had told her that her life was dangerous. She had done everything to stop her joining in this alien madness. But Maria had ignored the warnings. Of course she had. And some day she was going to get hurt, it was inevitable. But Sarah Jane meant what she had said – there was *always* a chance. And if they were going to find it and take it, they were going to have to talk to Mr Smith.

The computer needed a metabolic scan of Alan Jackson. Maria said she would do it. Sarah Jane knew that doing something practical towards helping her petrified father would help her deal with the situation better than any amount of crying. It only took a couple of minutes to run the scanner over her dad. Its data was transmitted instantly to Mr Smith and by the time she got back into the attic he had already analysed it.

'Mr Jackson has undergone massive molecular transmutation,' he was saying as she walked through the door.

'We know that. He's been turned to stone,' Sarah Jane snapped. Her patience was thin (not only had Alan been turned to stone but Luke and Clyde were still being held at the abbey, and she didn't want to imagine what might happen to them if she didn't get to them soon).

'Not stone,' said Mr Smith. 'Not strictly speaking. It's an organic petrification process.'

'Like fossilization,' Maria offered.

'It is comparable. And, to correct you again, Sarah Jane, Mr Jackson hasn't turned, but is *turning*.'

Sarah Jane was electrified, 'Do you mean the process isn't complete? It could still be reversed?'

'Theoretically', said Mr Smith. The molecular transmutation wasn't yet stable. That meant it could be reversed. But, he told them, he didn't know how to do it.

Maria felt like she was going crazy, 'Then you've got to work it out! You've got to save my Dad. Please, Mr Smith.'

'I'm not sure that there is sufficient time. My scan suggests the process will be complete in ninety minutes.'

Maria looked at her watch. It was 2.30. If Mr Smith didn't work this out by 4 o'clock her dad would be a statue for keeps. Sarah Jane saw the agony in her eyes.

'Please, Mr Smith,' Sarah Jane pleaded, 'you've got to help us.'

Mr Smith considered, 'Perhaps if I was more familiar with the Gorgon...'

Maria felt new hope surge through her. 'Bea! She might know something!'

Sarah Jane didn't want to crush Maria's hopes; she might, but...'Bea has Alzheimer's. Her mind is trapped in the past.'

But Maria wasn't going to let go of this shred of hope. 'It doesn't matter,' she said. 'That's where she met the Gorgon!'

And Sarah Jane knew she was right. Like she said, there was always a chance. They left the attic and rushed to the car.

At around the same time Luke was turning the pages of one of the books in the abbey library, occasionally glancing up to see Clyde pacing the room's length. Clyde didn't know how many times he'd gone from wall to wall since Sarah Jane and Maria had gone off with Sister Helena and the Gorgon.

'What's happening, Luke? Is Sarah Jane really going to give that Gorgon-thing the talisman?'

''Course not,' Luke told him, turning the pages and taking in every word with little more than a glance. 'If the Gorgon only wanted to go home, why would Mrs Nelson-Stanley have been so scared of the nuns finding the talisman? Mum knows that, she'll find some way of tricking them.'

And get us out of here? Clyde hoped.

'All the same, you and me – we should be looking for a way of escaping,' he told Luke. 'Not catching up on our reading.'

'It's a history of the abbey,' Luke said. 'Originally it was a private house, built in the sixteenth Century.'

'Bangin',' said Clyde. He could get a history lesson any time he wanted off Mrs Pittman, a teacher who looked so old she had probably witnessed most of what she taught.

But Luke was in the groove now. The house had been built at the time of the Reformation, Luke was telling him. King Henry VIII had declared himself head of a new English Church and under his daughter, Elizabeth I, priests and followers of the Catholic Church found themselves being persecuted.

'But what the Catholics used to do was build secret rooms and passages in their houses so that priests could hold their services in secret, and escape,' said Luke. He was making his way to the library's over-sized fireplace as he spoke, 'The people that built this house were Catholic.'

And he pushed on a stone in the fireplace and smiled when he felt it give. An instant later the back of the fireplace slid aside revealing a deep, dark tunnel.

Clyde's jaw dropped in amazement and awe, 'Are you good, or what?'

Luke crouched in the opening of the secret tunnel, 'It's very dark. It could be dangerous.'

'And hanging around here isn't? Come on.'

So Clyde led the way into the tunnel and Luke followed. It wasn't too bad for the first few steps, the light from the library cast a half-light ahead of them, and then Clyde felt a brick in the floor give beneath his foot. It was the closing mechanism for the doorway in the fireplace. It slid shut behind them. Now the darkness was total.

'Lovely,' said Clyde.

'Not afraid of the dark, are you?' asked Luke.

'Not the dark. Just what might be hiding in it.'

All the same, he pushed on, feeling carefully with his fingers, one hand on the wall to his side, the other held in front of him. The bricks on the wall felt damp and sometimes his fingers touched something slimy that clung to them. Clyde tried hard not to cry out like a girl. He managed fine until he somehow got himself wrapped up in about 300 years' worth of spider webs. Luke hissed at him to stop yelling – from the slope of the tunnel he figured they were now underneath the abbey somewhere, but Clyde's cry of shock and surprise as he walked into the spider webs would be carried through the tunnel's brickwork. The nuns might hear them! Clyde wiped spider web off his face and thought he felt hundreds of tiny legs running through his hair, but bit down on the urge to cry out again. Luke felt his way around Clyde then, and took the lead through the tunnel. They hadn't gone much further however when he saw a sliver of daylight ahead, and they made their way towards it.

The tunnel led them into some sort of forgotten outbuilding in the grounds of the abbey. It was filled with gardening tools that no one had used in decades. Creepers had found their way in through the broken window and wrapped themselves around the unused implements, like Nature had a sense of irony. The door to the outbuilding was locked, but the wood was flimsy and rotten, it didn't hold for long against the force of the two boys' shoulders. Then they were filling their lungs with fresh air and taking a moment to bask in warm sunshine again.

Clyde saw Luke move around the side of the old potting shed as he dusted himself off, and ran his fingers through his hair, hoping he had imagined those spiders up there. Quickly satisfied, he followed Luke – and what he saw brought him to a sudden stop.

They were behind the abbey, in its gardens. Despite the condition of the tools in the potting shed, someone was obviously taking care of the lawns and the neatly clipped hedges. But that wasn't what had Clyde rooted to the spot. Spread through the garden were statues. Dozens of them. And instinctively he knew that none of them had been carved by a sculptor – no artist would sculpt the kind of horror that Clyde saw on the faces of these statues. Once these had been people. They were the victims of the Gorgon.

Clyde found his voice and spoke to Luke, who stood just a couple of steps ahead of him, fascinated by the statues, 'Couldn't they get garden gnomes like everyone else?'

Luke didn't laugh, 'It's killed all these people, then put them on show like trophies. Or a warning.'

'Yeah,' said Clyde. 'And I'm taking it. Let's get out of here.'

Luke nodded and followed Clyde. They were going to have to go past the abbey itself to get through the gates, but it seemed quiet enough out here. Maybe the nuns had more to do today than tend their garden and statue collection.

They hid when the big black hearse pulled up.

Sister Helena got out of the car first, the Abbess

stepped out after her, as other nuns came through the front door of the abbey. Luke gasped when he saw Sister Helena brandish the talisman.

'We have the key!' she proclaimed. 'Rejoice, Sisters! The Gorgon shall be free!'

Sister Helena and the Abbess began to move towards the abbey, but as she reached the door the veiled nun stumbled badly and had to be caught and supported by Sister Helena and another nun. Sister Helena's brow furrowed, 'She is weakening. We must open the portal as soon as possible.'

Clyde and Luke watched as the nuns moved inside and the door thudded shut behind them.

'Right. Now, while the coast is clear!' Clyde had almost taken his first running step before he felt Luke's hand pull him back under cover.

'I can't,' said Luke.

'What you talking about?' Clyde hissed.

'I promised Mrs Nelson-Stanley I wouldn't let them get the talisman. I've let her down.'

Clyde drew a breath, 'When you promised her, did she tell you you'd be going up against a Gorgon and if you kept your word you'd probably end up a garden ornament?'

'Well – no, but...'

'She wasn't straight with you, Luke, and this

goes way beyond the call...'

'Mum would never have given them the talisman – unless something had happened.'

Clyde had seen Sister Helena holding the talisman. He had been trying to ignore the uncomfortable questions that conjured up about Sarah Jane and Maria.

Luke's eyes were set with determination, 'I'm not going to let the Gorgon win, Clyde. I'm just not. But I'm going to need your help.'

Like Clyde had any choice.

Chapter Eleven

Host

Maria stood outside Bea Nelson-Stanley's door. She heard music. Someone singing about having a pocketful of starlight. Sarah Jane had apologised as she drove to Lavender Lawns, she wasn't going to be able to go in with Maria. She had to find Luke and Clyde. Maria understood.

'Everything Bea knows about the Gorgon is still inside her head,' Sarah Jane said, pushing the little blue car for everything it would give her. 'You just have to find a way to unlock it.'

When they reached the rest home, Sarah Jane hugged Maria and wished her luck. Then she said, 'You were right, I never should have let any of you get involved. It's not just you or me that gets threatened by all this alien madness. It's everyone we know.'

Maria had seen tears in Sarah Jane's eyes, and she felt wretched for what she had said earlier, 'It's not your fault. I wanted to see aliens. Who wouldn't?'

Sarah Jane smiled, then fixed her with steely eyes, 'If there's a way of saving your dad, I know you're going to do it!'

And then she was gone. And now Maria was standing outside Bea's door. And she was wondering just how on earth was she going to do this?

Catch a shooting star
And put it in your pocket
Save it for a rainy day...

Maria knocked on the door. But she got no answer, just the guy singing on Bea's old record player.

For when your troubles start multiplyin'
And they just might!
It's easy to forget them without tryin'
With just a pocketful of starlight!

Maria looked at her watch, it was 2.45. Fifteen

minutes gone, already! She twisted the door handle and walked in. Bea didn't notice, she was happily singing along to the record.

'Bea? Hello, it's Maria. Do you remember me?'

Bea stopped singing and looked at her, suddenly puzzled, 'Hello, darling, you're a little young, aren't you?'

Maria felt her heart sink. Bea didn't remember her.

'Young?' she asked.

'Yes, dear. To be curator of the Museum of Egyptology.'

Maria fought the tears that she felt burning behind her eyes as she felt time running out with every passing second.

The nuns had gathered in the great hall of the abbey. At its centre lay what looked like a well carved from ancient stone surrounded by Grecian pillars. The Abbess was now in a wheelchair. She held the talisman in one clawed hand and it glowed again – ice-blue.

Sister Helena gazed at the other nuns. 'Sisters, after 3,000 years our work comes to an end. And our world is on the threshold of a new age.'

The well-shaped construction in the middle of

the room was the Gorgon's portal, protected like the creature itself over the millennia, and now soon to come to life again for the first time in thousands of years. Sister Helena knew that the Gorgon world was a million light years away– it would take maybe an hour for the angles of ascension to align and the portal to open. When it did, those billions of miles across space would be nothing but a footstep. She wheeled the Abbess towards the portal and one clawed hand put the talisman in place. A glow began to develop at the centre of the portal.

'Sisters, the portal is opening. In an hour the portal will open and after all these centuries the Abbess's people will join her and the Gorgons will have their promised land!'

Suddenly the Abbess reached out, grabbing Sister Helena's arm. The talons dug into her flesh with urgency.

Time grows short!

Sister Helena heard the creature's voice in her head, and she understood what she had to do.

'The host is dying,' she said. 'We must find a new carrier before the portal opens.'

Maria looked at the clock on Bea's mantelpiece.

Another ten minutes had dragged by, and she had got nowhere. She watched Bea put another record on her old player.

'Bea,' she said, 'please help me. You have to tell me about the Gorgon.'

But Bea was swaying to the music. Maria recognised it as Perry Como again. The guy who had been singing about shooting stars and putting them in your pocket. Bea had told her that much. Big deal.

Bea's eyes were closed, she was smiling dreamily, 'Edgar and I danced to this once in the palace of the...' she struggled for a moment, fighting with some part of her brain that refused to give her what she wanted, 'The Sultan of Ishkanbah. Do you know the Sultan?'

Maria felt like screaming. Somehow she hung on to her temper, 'No. I've never even heard of Ishkanwherever. Listen, Bea, the Gorgon has turned my dad into stone, and if you don't help me, I'm never going to get him back. Do you understand?'

But Bea was in another world, 'The Sultan was such a fascinating man. He had seen the Yeti, you know? He was one of the few people Edgar and I could really talk to about the things we had seen.'

Maria felt a spark of new hope. 'Tell me about the things you've seen. I've seen all kinds of things with Sarah Jane. She's seen loads of aliens and monsters on Earth, even other planets. She's had hundreds of adventures, just like you and Edgar did.'

Bea stopped swaying with the music and sat down. She didn't look dreamy any more, she looked sad. 'Edgar, I loved him so much, and he's been gone so long. What I wouldn't give to hear his voice just once more.'

She looked at Maria, and smiled again, but it was still sad, 'We had adventures once, such adventures. But no one believes me now. No one listens to you when you're old.'

'I believe you, Bea!'

But Bea's eyes had wandered to the window, and her mind had flown to another age.

'*Bea!*'

Clyde looked at his watch, it was forty-five seconds off 3 o'clock. He hoped Luke was in place. He looked up at the rope that hung down in front of him. He hoped he could do this okay.

Five seconds later, Luke checked his watch. He

had used what he remembered from the book on the abbey's history to negotiate his way through its network of secret passages, and now he was hidden behind a tapestry in the great hall. He could see the nuns gathered around the portal which glowed ever-brighter. He heard one of the nuns say something about alignment being at forty-five per cent and Sister Helena said that was good. Another nun asked about the Abbess – Luke noted that she wasn't with the others in the hall.

'Her strength is failing,' said Sister Helena. 'Soon we will select a new host.'

Host? Luke wondered, what was that all about?

'Soon the Gorgons and humanity will be one.'

And in the abbey bell tower, that was when Clyde's watch turned to exactly 3 o'clock and he started hauling on the bell rope.

The sound of the bell rang through the great hall.

Sister Helena's eyes flashed, 'What on Earth...?' She turned on the other nuns, 'Find out what's going on!'

And as the nuns rushed out, Luke took his chance and bolted from the cover of the tapestry.

He saw the talisman on the portal and lunged for it, grabbed it. But in the same instant the double doors of the great hall flew open – Luke saw the Abbess in a wheelchair framed by the doorway, but didn't hang around. He ran for the door at the other end of the room as the Abbess raised her veil. Luke heard the Gorgon make a horrific noise and instinctively ducked as serpents of blue light hit the chair that he hid behind. He saw it turn instantly to stone. Luke ran again and threw himself through the door. As he slammed it behind him, the Gorgon's light serpents struck it and it was transformed.

Luke ran through the abbey. The history book had left him with a perfect mental plan of the abbey, and he didn't need to stop and think. Moments later he burst through the front door and was running down the steps. He saw Clyde running towards him.

'You got it?' Clyde shouted.

Luke held up the talisman in answer.

But that was when they saw the nuns.

They seemed to come from everywhere. Dozens of them. They didn't run, but they didn't need to – there were just so many. They moved steadily, almost seeming to float in those black gowns over the ground.

'They're everywhere,' Luke gasped.

And they were.

'Quick! This way!'

Luke and Clyde turned and saw Sarah Jane. She was on foot near the woodland that bordered the abbey grounds. But even as they ran towards her, more nuns emerged from the trees, and in moments they were surrounded, the nuns crowding around them, hemming them in. There was no escape.

Then as if by silent command, some of the nuns moved aside to reveal Sister Helena. She stared at Sarah Jane with cold eyes and smiled, 'Sarah Jane Smith, how convenient of you to drop by.'

The nuns locked them in the cellar. There was no chance to make a run for it. Not then. Sarah Jane knew an opportunity would come along, it always did. But the chances of escape took a nosedive when the nuns took her bag – and the sonic lipstick with it – before slamming the heavy old cellar door on them.

The loss of the sonic lipstick didn't concern Clyde much, however. He was rapping at the cellar walls, trying to find another secret passage. Luke had read all about them, he told Sarah

Jane confidently, he had them all stored in that superbrain of his. But Luke didn't recall any down here. He had other things on his mind.

'Mum, I think the Gorgon is dying,' he said.

Sarah Jane raised an eyebrow, 'What makes you think that?'

'We saw her stumble, like she was sick,' said Clyde, breaking off from his wall tapping.

'And I heard Sister Helena talking about them having to find a new host. And she said something about that when the portal opened humanity and the Gorgons would be one.'

Sarah Jane suddenly felt ill. So that was what the Gorgons wanted with Earth! Back in Bannerman Road, Sister Helena had said the Gorgons needed humanity in order to survive, but Sarah Jane had never imagined just what kind of nightmare that meant...

That was when the cellar door opened. A couple of nuns had come to take Sarah Jane to Sister Helena. Sarah Jane told Luke and Clyde not to worry, she would be fine. She wasn't sure that she believed it – but at least she wasn't going to be locked in the cellar any more, that had to be an improvement on the current situation.

The nuns took her to the great hall, where the

talisman was once again installed on the portal which now glowed with bright light. Sister Helena was waiting for her along with the Abbess in her wheelchair.

'What makes you think the Gorgons will still want to invade?' asked Sarah Jane as she was led in. 'Three thousand years is a long time.'

'Not for the Gorgons.'

'Without host bodies to carry them? The Gorgons are parasites, aren't they? A life form that lives on another. That depends on it to feed and survive. Your Abbess was human once, wasn't she?'

Sister Helena spoke with pride, 'The Gorgon gives its host life beyond human years. The Abbess has carried the Gorgon for 200 years. But there have been many hosts over the generations, and now she grows weak.

'Her time is coming, and the Gorgon has chosen a new host to lead its domination of Earth.'

Sister Helena stared at Sarah Jane, 'You, Miss Smith.'

Chapter Twelve

The statue that cried

Chrissie had had quite enough.

First Maria had thrown a hissy fit and stomped out on her. And what had she done? Just shown a bit of maternal concern for the company she was keeping. That's all.

Then Alan had taken a pop. Said she was insensitive turning up on their doorstep the way she had. Well, yes, she knew she hadn't been the perfect mum, but Maria was still her daughter, and she had every right to spend some time with her. It was just coincidence that she and Ivan were on a bit of a break.

Yeah, come to think of it, there was Ivan as

well, wasn't there? And Carlos, the salsa teacher.

Blokes!

Didn't matter how much hair gel and moisturizer they used, underneath they were still just cavemen.

But at least she had walked out on Ivan. Now it looked like Alan had followed in Maria's stroppy footsteps and done a runner.

After they'd had their barney, Alan had said he was going to look for Maria. That had been hours ago. It wasn't like it was going to be that tough to find her; she was going to be with Calamity Jane across the road, wasn't she?

Chrissie reckoned Calamity Jane had got her sights set on Alan. It wasn't Maria she was interested in at all, she'd just befriended her to worm her way in with her hunky old man. Chrissie had to admit to herself that Alan was still quite a hunk, even compared to Ivan...and Carlos. And she was pretty flaming sure that's where she was going to find the two of them now!

Well, Chrissie had had quite enough. And now she was hammering on Calamity Jane's front door.

No one answered.

Chrissie did what every suspicious mum and

wife did. Even ex-wives. She shouted through the letterbox.

'Maria? Are you in there? Alan?'

Still no answer.

So she opened the gate and went around the back and peered through the window.

She didn't quite know what she expected to see.

She never expected to see a statue of Alan in Calamity Jane's lounge.

Chrissie's brain reeled. What sort of a woman was she dealing with here?

Obsessed!

She had read about women like this in her magazines.

The window opened to her touch and Chrissie, heart-in-mouth, unsure of exactly what she was planning to do, but knowing there was no way she could just walk away from this statue of her husband, climbed into the lounge.

It was uncanny, she thought, as she stood before it, it almost felt like Alan was in the room. If Sarah Jane had sculpted this, then she had done a good job. She really had him. Maybe taken a bit off his bum, but she supposed that was – *what was it they call it?* – artistic licence.

'Suppose you'd be flattered if you knew, wouldn't you?' she said to the statue. 'Always did fancy yourself a bit, didn't you?'

But maybe he did know – maybe Alan had posed for Sarah Jane.

'No,' Chrissie shook her head as she looked him over. 'You wouldn't pose in them old jeans and trainers, would you? And she'd want to get you in the all-together, wouldn't she? Cheeky old...'

Then Chrissie caught hold of herself, 'So is this what it's come to? Talking to a flaming statue instead of the real thing?

'Maybe her and me aren't so different. Both of us have to make do with what we can. Difference is, she doesn't know what she's missing, does she?'

The statue seemed to be giving her a look – like it was all her fault.

'I know,' she told it. 'I should have tried more. Should have done more, listened more...what do you want me to say? The world doesn't revolve around me? Yeah, I get it. Now.

'Still, you're all right – you and Maria. Better off without me around messing things up. Well, like I said, I can make do. That's 'til I mess up again. Which I will, of course, 'cos I'm me, aren't I?'

She sighed, realised how ridiculous she must look, and went over to the window, ready to leave the way she had come.

She turned back to Alan once more, 'Anyway, been nice talking to you.' Then she left.

She didn't see the single tear that fell from the statue's eye.

Chapter Thirteen

Twenty past three

'Sarah Jane was right, wasn't she? I thought meeting creatures from other planets was going to be exciting and cool...but she told me, she said it wasn't anything like that.

'In the end it just messes you up. Your whole life. And the people you love.'

Maria was fighting back tears as she spoke to Bea without knowing whether she could hear her or not. The old woman sat gazing out of the window the way she seemed to have been for ages. The clock on her mantelpiece said it was twenty past three. Maria had just forty minutes to save her father.

'That's why Sarah Jane's on her own,' Maria continued. 'That's why you're here, isn't it? With no one in the world that really cares.

'This is how we all end up, isn't it?'

She almost jumped when Bea's fingers wrapped around her hand. 'I had my Edgar,' said Bea. 'You're young, you will find yours.'

Maria looked into the old woman's eyes, and felt her heart beating fast, 'Bea! Are you really there?'

'What sort of a question is that? Where else would I be?'

Maria beamed with relief, 'Bea, I haven't got much time. The Gorgon – it's turned my dad to stone. Is there a way to save him?'

Bea's fingers went to her mouth, a gesture of horror, 'Your father? Oh, dear. Oh, deary-dear. That's – that's most unpleasant.'

Maria saw Bea's narrow shoulders shudder. 'I should know,' she continued, 'it did it to me, you know.'

Maria couldn't believe it – Bea had been turned to stone, and survived! She could have screamed with joy.

'Those nuns,' Bea said. 'They came after the talisman.'

'But Edgar saved you. He must have. How?'

'The talisman,' she said, prising the word out from an ungenerous brain. 'It is the key to the doorway between this world and theirs. But it is more. It returned me to flesh and blood.'

The talisman! Maria saw all those sudden hopes of saving her father spiral to the ground like dead leaves on an autumn breeze.

'The talisman,' she said. 'The Gorgon's got it.'

Bea's eyes blazed, 'Then you have to get it back! Not just for your father – for every soul on Earth!'

Maria set her jaw with determination, of course she did, and she would. To save the planet, but first of all, to save her dad.

'Thank you, Bea,' she said, and jumped up.

But Bea grabbed her hand, 'Not so fast, young lady! Reach my...' her lips tried to shape the word. Her eyes flared with anger, 'For goodness' sake! My mirror! Get my mirror.'

She indicated a small mirror with a silver handle on the nearby dressing table. Maria took it and handed it to Bea. It was the least she could do, she thought. But Bea shook her head, 'I don't want it! What do you think I'm going to do? Comb my hair while you take on that monster?

It's for you!'

Maria didn't understand, she looked from Bea to the hand mirror and shook her head, 'For me?'

Bea rolled her eyes impatiently, 'Whatever do they teach you in school these days?'

Chapter Fourteen

Serve the Gorgon

Luke had been right – there were no secret passages to offer an escape from the locked cellar. But that didn't mean they weren't going to get out of there. Whatever was going on upstairs, whatever Sister Helena and the Abbess were doing with Sarah Jane, he and Clyde were going to get out of there. And he was going to do it with an old flat trowel that he found among the rubbish down there.

Clyde was unimpressed, 'You're going to dig a tunnel?'

'No,' Luke told him. 'I'm going to make a screwdriver. The old fashioned kind.'

Upstairs, the Abbess hadn't moved for some time. Sarah Jane had been watching her, and watching the light from the portal grow in intensity. The nuns had tied her up, but that didn't mean she was ready to give in to the horrible fate the nuns and their Gorgon mistress planned for her.

'Not long now, Miss Smith,' said Sister Helena. 'As the Abbess weakens more the Gorgon will release its hold on her and you will become leader of a new race ruling Planet Earth.'

'You can do what you want to me,' Sarah Jane growled, 'but this planet will never bow down to that *thing!*'

Sister Helena sneered, 'It will. And so will you.'

Sarah Jane strained against the ropes that bound her. There was no way it was going to end like this, she told herself. No way. But the ropes wouldn't give. Her only hope, she knew, lay with the boys. If only they could find a way to escape!

And at that moment Luke's makeshift screwdriver was removing the last screw on the lock mechanism of the cellar door. Clyde watched over his shoulder and passed Luke a rusty old nail that he had found while Luke worked on the screws. Luke used the nail to fiddle inside the mechanism for a moment or two as Clyde held his breath.

If this doesn't work...

And then the lock sprang open.

The boys exchanged a grin, then stepped cautiously out into the corridor. No sign of any nuns – *yet*.

'We need a plan,' said Luke.

But Clyde was already making his way up the old stone steps, 'Yeah, sure. When we'll get the chance we'll work one out. Meantime, we've got to find Sarah Jane.'

'The great hall,' said Luke. 'That's where they've got the portal. She'll be there. Come on.'

And Luke knew exactly what he was looking for – another secret tunnel.

Meanwhile, Sarah Jane was watching the glow of the portal carefully. It had begun to change. Other lights were beginning to swim and swirl in the glow. She felt the slightest breeze touch her face. She felt it grow stronger.

The portal was close to opening.

Sister Helena's face was alive with excitement, 'The Gorgons are coming! Their new queen must be ready to meet them!'

Sarah Jane felt the nun's eyes fall on her, 'Bring the host forward.'

Sarah Jane wasn't about to scream, or beg for mercy, but there was no way she was going to go easily, either and she struggled as two nuns drew her to face the Abbess in her wheelchair.

'Don't struggle, Miss Smith,' Sister Helena preached. 'Embrace your destiny.'

'The Gorgon is controlling you,' Sarah Jane told her. 'It's controlling all of you! You have to fight it! If you don't, they'll come through that portal and destroy all the human race!'

But Sister Helena was unmoved, 'No. The Gorgons will save us. From wars, from greed. We will exist only to serve them. We will be at peace everlasting. And you will be our queen!'

The nuns around Sarah Jane began to chant.

Serve the Gorgon! Serve the Gorgon!

From behind her, another nun put a blindfold around Sarah Jane's eyes.

'What are you doing?' she demanded.

'If you saw the Gorgon as it transferred its essence to you, you would be turned to stone, Miss Smith. We wouldn't want that. And neither would you.'

Sarah Jane snarled defiantly, 'I'd rather end my

days as a lump of granite than carry around that abomination in my head!'

And that's when Luke and Clyde broke from their cover behind a tapestry and charged towards Sarah Jane and the nuns that held her. Clyde bowled two of the nuns over and Luke had his hands on Sarah Jane's bindings before other nuns grabbed them.

Sister Helena clapped mockingly, 'The cavalry to the rescue, I don't think.'

'I'm sorry, Sarah Jane,' said Luke. And she felt her heart break.

'Hold them,' said Sister Helena. 'They will be the first prey for our new queen.'

'No!' cried Sarah Jane. 'Boys, don't look. Close your eyes. Whatever you do, don't look!'

And Sister Helena lifted the Abbess's veil.

The snake lights poured out of the old, shrivelled woman, a torrent of writhing blue lights that spun through the air towards blindfolded Sarah Jane...

The others averted their eyes.

And no one saw Maria burst through the doors of the great hall and lurch towards the Gorgon, keeping her eyes fixed on Bea's mirror and the reflected image of the room, before throwing herself in the way of the snake-lights and turning the mirror on them.

'Rock on!' she screamed.

In a burst of unearthly blue light, the snake-lights were reflected back at themselves and the Abbess. There was a hideous scream and suddenly the lights had gone. In their place was the Abbess turned to stone.

Luke cried out, 'Maria! You've done it! You've killed it!' In the same moment he found he was able to break away from the nun that held him. Clyde was free too, and tore the blindfold away from Sarah Jane, then began to untie her.

Around them the nuns seemed lost, disoriented.

Sister Helena was looking around her, frightened, 'Where am I? What happened?'

Clyde got Sarah Jane free; she took Sister Helena's shoulders, 'The Gorgon has lost its control over you. You're free.'

But it wasn't over yet.

The room was filled with the hideous wail of Gorgons. More Gorgons. Hundreds of them.

Clyde turned towards the portal, 'They're coming through!'

And in its glow they could see writhing snake-like shapes growing stronger.

Maria threw herself at the portal and tore the talisman from it. Instantly the light died, and with it the sound of the Gorgons.

Sarah Jane wrapped her arms around Maria, and hugged her tight.

'But, what about your father?'

Maria looked at her watch – it was 3.45.

'Come on,' she gasped. 'Quick!'

Chapter Fifteen

Wonderful things

They stood in a ring around the stone statue that had once been Alan Jackson. Maria held the talisman in one hand. Clyde looked at his watch.

'You've only got a couple of minutes.'

But Maria hesitated, 'What if it doesn't work?'

'If it saved Bea, it will save your father,' said Sarah Jane.

Maria bit her lip and refused to imagine anything but the power of the talisman transforming her father back to flesh and blood. She took a breath and placed the chain around the statue's neck. The talisman lay on Alan's chest and began to glow instantly. A moment later its light spread out, wrapping around the statue, shimmering and swirling. And then Alan fell to the floor, flesh and blood once more but unconscious.

When he came to a little while later he was alone, lying on the bench in Sarah Jane's garden. He looked around him, confused, his head throbbing. *How did I get here?*

He picked himself up. His joints ached like old, unoiled machinery, but he got himself going. He felt fine by the time he got to his own kitchen door – but he still had no idea how he had wound up asleep in Sarah Jane's garden. The last thing he remembered was looking for Maria.

Stepping in to the kitchen he found Chrissie. She was scowling, which was bad. Her bags were packed, which was good.

'Where the heck have you been? I've been out looking for you. It's been ages!'

'I fell asleep,' he told her. 'Must have been over-doing it lately.'

Maria came through the door.

'Oh,' Chrissie cried. 'Another one of the Disappearing Jacksons!'

But Maria ignored her, throwing her arms around Alan, 'Dad!'

'Maria,' he said, 'I'm so sorry about earlier.'

'No, Dad. I'm really sorry. I thought I'd lost you!'

He gave her a puzzled smile, 'Don't be silly. It was only a tiff. You're never going to lose me.'

Chrissie watched, feeling excluded. Time for her quid's worth, 'Maria, do you know what that woman over the road has in her lounge?'

Maria knew what Chrissie meant straight away, though she couldn't believe that her mother had actually been snooping around Sarah Jane's house. Well, if she'd seen a statue of Alan, it wasn't going to be there now, was it?

As Chrissie hauled Maria and Alan across the road, Maria tried to tell her mum that she must have been seeing things, but Chrissie wasn't in any mood to listen. And when Sarah Jane opened the door to her, Chrissie all but forced her way into the house and stormed into the lounge...

But all she found were Luke and Clyde playing *Alien Devastation 3*. There was no statue.

Chrissie's eyes were round with disbelief.

'Pity really,' said Alan. 'Do you think I'd look good as one of those Greek statues, Maria?'

He struck a pose and Maria told him she preferred him just the way he was. Then somehow they got Chrissie out of there, still protesting that she had seen a statue and demanding to know what Sarah Jane had done with it.

But it was the last straw for Chrissie. Her bags were already packed and she got Alan to call her a cab as soon as they were back over the road. She told them that she had had Ivan on the phone earlier in floods, begging her to come home. What else could she do? But as she got into the taxi she told Maria again that she knew what she had seen over the road, and she warned her for the second time that day that there was something weird about Calamity Jane. Maria didn't get mad this time, she hugged her mum and told her that she loved her.

Later that evening, Maria returned to Sarah Jane's and found her with Luke in the attic. He had some questions about the talisman, which he fingered curiously, its green glow playing across his face.

'If the talisman was the key to the Gorgon's portal, how come it could also turn Mr Jackson back to flesh and blood?'

Mr Smith was out of the wall. Since the talisman had been returned to him he had been able to complete his analysis, 'All matter has an atomic default. Some alien technology – including that of the Gorgons – uses this default to turn things on and off. Such technology can reverse cellular distortion.'

A light went on in Maria's head, 'You mean it can make things the way they used to be?' She turned to Sarah Jane, excited, 'Maybe it could help Bea!'

But Sarah Jane was doubtful, 'Maria, Bea has Alzheimer's. Besides she had the talisman all that time.'

'In a tin box,' Luke said. 'Maybe she hasn't actually touched the talisman in all these years.'

Maria was determined. 'She helped save my dad, Sarah Jane. Please, we have to try. Like you said, there is always a chance.'

Sarah Jane smiled. Yes, there was always a chance. And perhaps Maria was right; they owed it to her to help Bea, if they could. And an hour later she and Maria were slipping into Bea's room at Lavender Lawns. She had Bing Crosby playing on the old record player, but she looked up and smiled a welcome. But Sarah Jane knew that didn't mean she knew who they were.

'Hello, Bea. It's Maria. I've brought something that belongs to you.'

'Oh, is it my compact?' Bea said. 'I'm always leaving it lying around. Edgar says I'll lose my head one of these days.'

'It's something Edgar gave you,' Maria told her, and revealed the talisman.

Bea's eyes glowed with recognition and sentimental memories, but they were pushed aside by fright, 'No! You must put it back where I hid it. Put it back! In case they come!'

But Sarah Jane took her hand, 'It's all right, Bea. The Sisters are never going to come looking for it again. The Gorgon is dead.'

A tear fell from Bea's eye, 'Is it true?'

Maria felt her own eyes filling with tears as she reassured Bea, and passed the talisman to her. Bea's long fingers clasped it to her chest, her eyes closed and more tears coursed down her slender cheeks.

'Edgar gave it to me,' she said. 'Oh, we saw such things together. Wonderful things. People made of light, mermaids leaping with dolphins, young Yetis frolicking in the snow...'

The smile that came with her wonderful memories began to fade, 'But he's been gone so long, and I've always been so scared to wear this.' She gazed at the talisman, it glowed dark green as her fingers caressed it. Maria felt herself holding her breath.

'You know,' said Bea, 'he put this around my neck, and kissed me for the very first time, and told me that he loved me.'

She slipped the chain over her head. The talisman settled on her breast, her hands around it. And Maria and Sarah Jane watched as the light within the talisman flickered and died. Bea didn't notice.

I will always love you, Bea.

She heard his voice. He had whispered in her ear, just as he had that first time. She heard it as clear as day. She knew that the girl and the woman with the auburn hair hadn't heard him. But that didn't matter, it didn't matter at all.

'Thank you for bringing him back to me,' she said.

And they left Bea with her memories.

They walked down the staircase from her room, and out on to the gravelled drive. It was a beautiful night. The sky had been sprayed with a million jewels. But Sarah Jane could see that Maria was disappointed, there had been no miraculous transformation, the talisman had been alien but it hadn't been magic.

'You shouldn't be upset,' Sarah Jane told Maria. 'The talisman didn't cure Bea, but it did something amazing, all the same. It gave her peace.'

Maria could see that. The talisman may not have been enchanted, but the look on the old lady's face as they left her had been magical.

'She was lucky, wasn't she?' said Maria. 'Having Edgar.'

'I suppose she was,' said Sarah Jane, digging the keys to the little blue car from her jacket.

Maria bit her lip, unsure of whether to say what she was thinking, and then found she was saying it anyway, 'Don't you wish you had found someone special to share it all with?'

Sarah Jane looked at her over the top of the car, and smiled. 'I think I have,' she said. 'For the second time.'

If life on earth with Sarah Jane is an adventure then try travelling in time with the Doctor!

Decide your destiny by choosing the direction the story will go....

Eight titles to collect with four new books publishing in March 2008